MARVEL SUPER HERO ADVENTURES

CAPTAIN MARVEL: FIRST DAY OF SCHOOL!

starring:
Spider-Man
Captain Marvel

A bite from a radioactive spider gave PETER PARKER the speed, strength, and agility of an arachnid! After learning that with great power there must also come great responsibility, he became the crimefighting super hero SPIDER-MAN.

CAROL DANVERS was a U.S. Air Force pilot until an alien machine gave her superhuman powers. Now, she flies high as she uses her strength, speed, and the ability to absorb and fire energy bolts to protect the world as Earth's Mightiest Hero: CAPTAIN MARVEL.

writer SHOLLY FISCH
artist MARIO DEL PENNINO
color artist JAVA TARTAGLIA
letterer VC's JOE CARAMAGNA
cover artists AGNES GARBOWSKA & CHRIS SOTOMAYOR

assistant editor LAUREN AMARO
editor DEVIN LEWIS
supervising editor SANA AMANAT
editor in chief C.B. CEBULSKI
chief creative officer JOE QUESADA
president DAN BUCKLEY
executive producer ALAN FINE

special thanks to DEREK LAUFMAN

ABDO Spotlight

ABDOBOOKS.COM

Reinforced library bound edition published in 2020 by Spotlight,
a division of ABDO, PO Box 398166, Minneapolis, Minnesota 55439.
Spotlight produces high-quality reinforced library bound editions for
schools and libraries. Published by agreement with Marvel Characters, Inc.

Printed in the United States of America, North Mankato, Minnesota.
092019
012020

THIS BOOK CONTAINS
RECYCLED MATERIALS

marvelkids.com
© 2020 MARVEL

Library of Congress Control Number: 2019942032

Publisher's Cataloging-in-Publication Data

Names: Fisch, Sholly; Templeton, Ty, authors. | Del Pennino, Mario; Tartaglia, Java;
    Templeton, Ty; Smith, Kieren, illustrators.
Title: Captain Marvel: first day of school! / by Sholly Fisch, and Ty Templeton;
    illustrated by Mario Del Pennino, Java Tartaglia, Ty Templeton and Kieren
    Smith.
Description: Minneapolis, Minnesota : Spotlight, 2020. | Series: Marvel super hero
    adventures graphic novels
Summary: Captain Marvel runs into trouble and has to work with Spider-Man to
    save the day.
Identifiers: ISBN 9781532144455 (lib. bdg.)
Subjects: LCSH: Captain Marvel (Fictitious character)--Juvenile fiction. |
    Superheroes--Juvenile fiction. | Spider-Man (Fictitious character)--Juvenile
    fiction. | Good and evil--Juvenile fiction. | Adventure stories--Juvenile fiction. |
    Graphic novels--Juvenile fiction. | Comic books, strips, etc.--Juvenile fiction.
Classification: DDC 741.5--dc23

Spotlight

A Division of ABDO
abdobooks.com

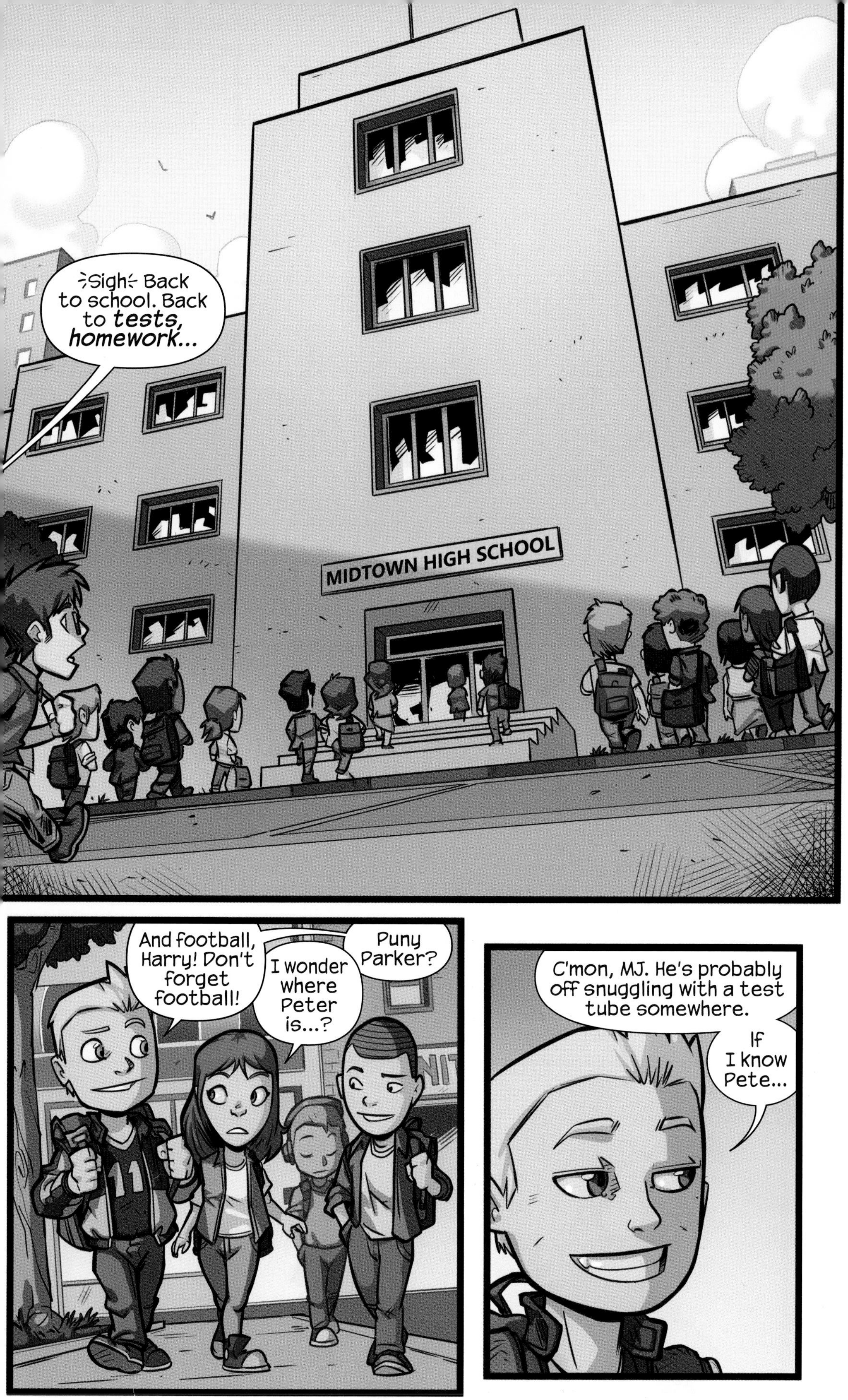

⁑Sigh⁑ Back to school. Back to *tests, homework...*
MIDTOWN HIGH SCHOOL
And football, Harry! Don't forget football!
Puny Parker?
I wonder where Peter is...?
C'mon, MJ. He's probably off snuggling with a test tube somewhere.
If I know Pete...

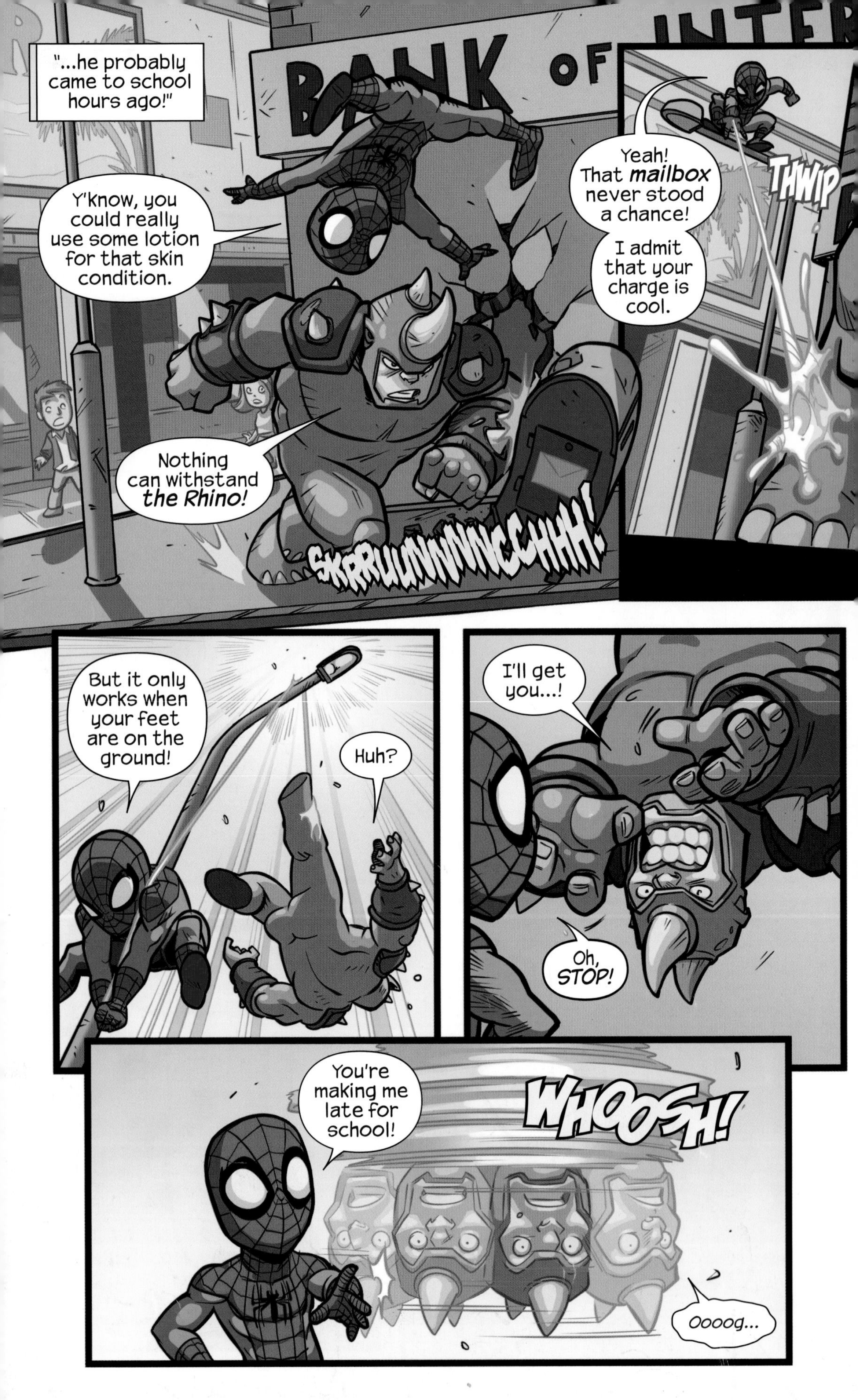

"...he probably came to school hours ago!"
BANK OF INTER
Y'know, you could really use some lotion for that skin condition.
Yeah! That *mailbox* never stood a chance!
I admit that your charge is cool.
THWIP
Nothing can withstand *the Rhino!*
SKRRUUNNNNNCHHH!
But it only works when your feet are on the ground!
Huh?
I'll get you...!
Oh, STOP!
You're making me late for school!
WHOOSH!
Oooog...

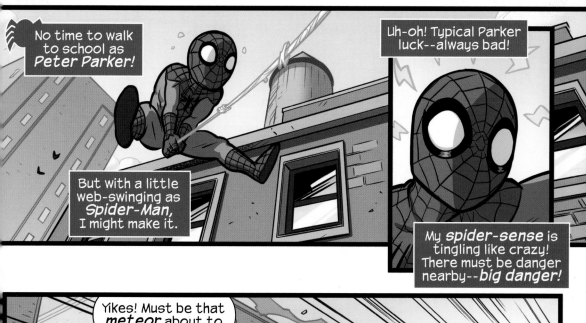

No time to walk to school as *Peter Parker!*

But with a little web-swinging as *Spider-Man,* I might make it.

Uh-oh! Typical Parker luck--always bad!

My *spider-sense* is tingling like crazy! There must be danger nearby--*big danger!*

Yikes! Must be that *meteor* about to hit the city...

...and my *SCHOOL!*

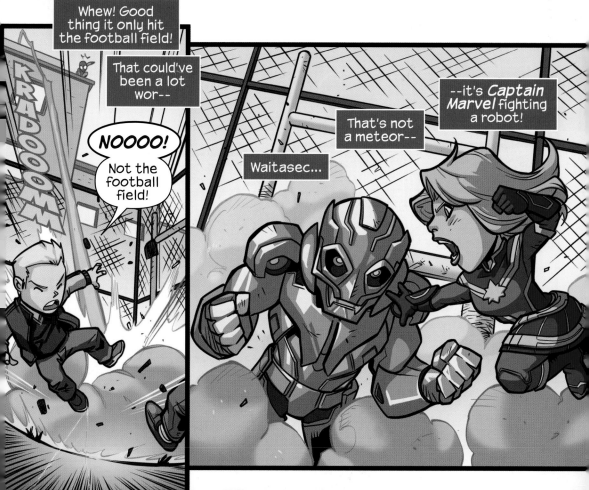

Whew! Good thing it only hit the football field!

That could've been a lot wor--

KRADOOOM

NOOOO!

Not the football field!

Waitasec...

That's not a meteor--

--it's *Captain Marvel* fighting a robot!

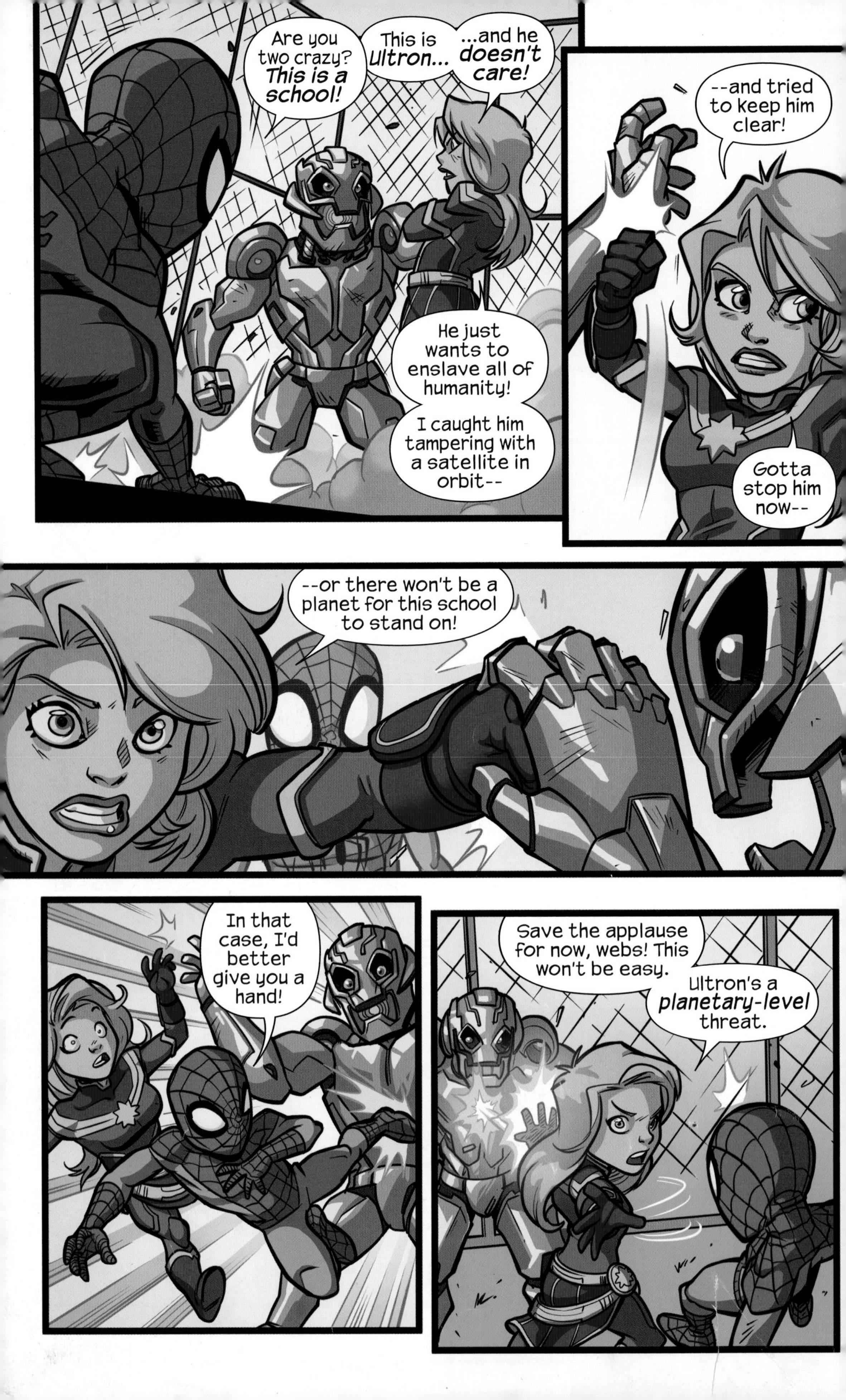
Are you two crazy? This is a school!
This is Ultron...
...and he doesn't care!
He just wants to enslave all of humanity!
I caught him tampering with a satellite in orbit--
--and tried to keep him clear!
Gotta stop him now--
--or there won't be a planet for this school to stand on!
In that case, I'd better give you a hand!
Save the applause for now, webs! This won't be easy.
Ultron's a planetary-level threat.

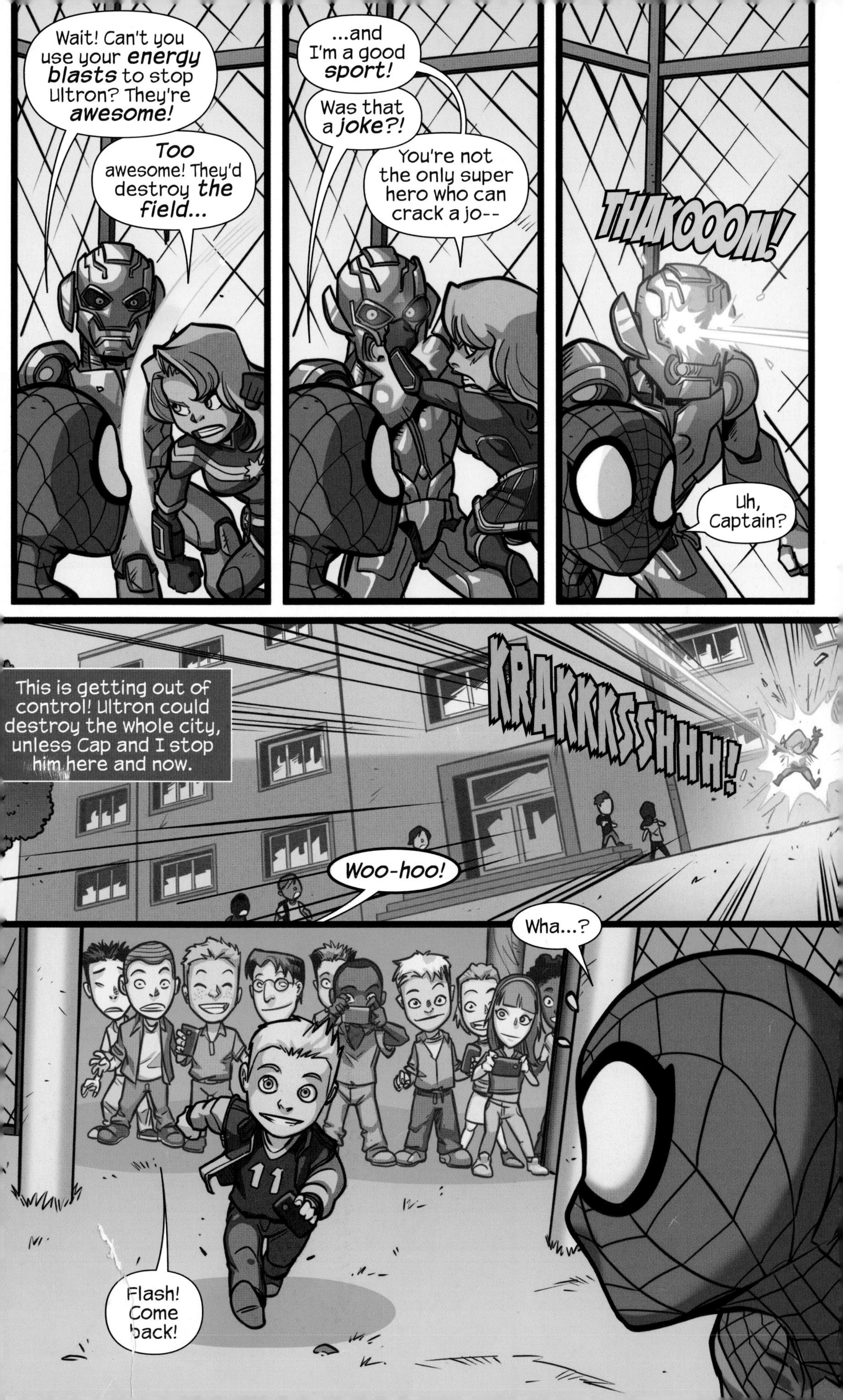
Wait! Can't you use your energy blasts to stop Ultron? They're awesome!
Too awesome! They'd destroy the field...
...and I'm a good sport!
Was that a joke?!
You're not the only super hero who can crack a jo--
THAKOOOM!
Uh, Captain?
This is getting out of control! Ultron could destroy the whole city, unless Cap and I stop him here and now.
KRAKKKSSHHH!
Woo-hoo!
Wha...?
Flash! Come back!

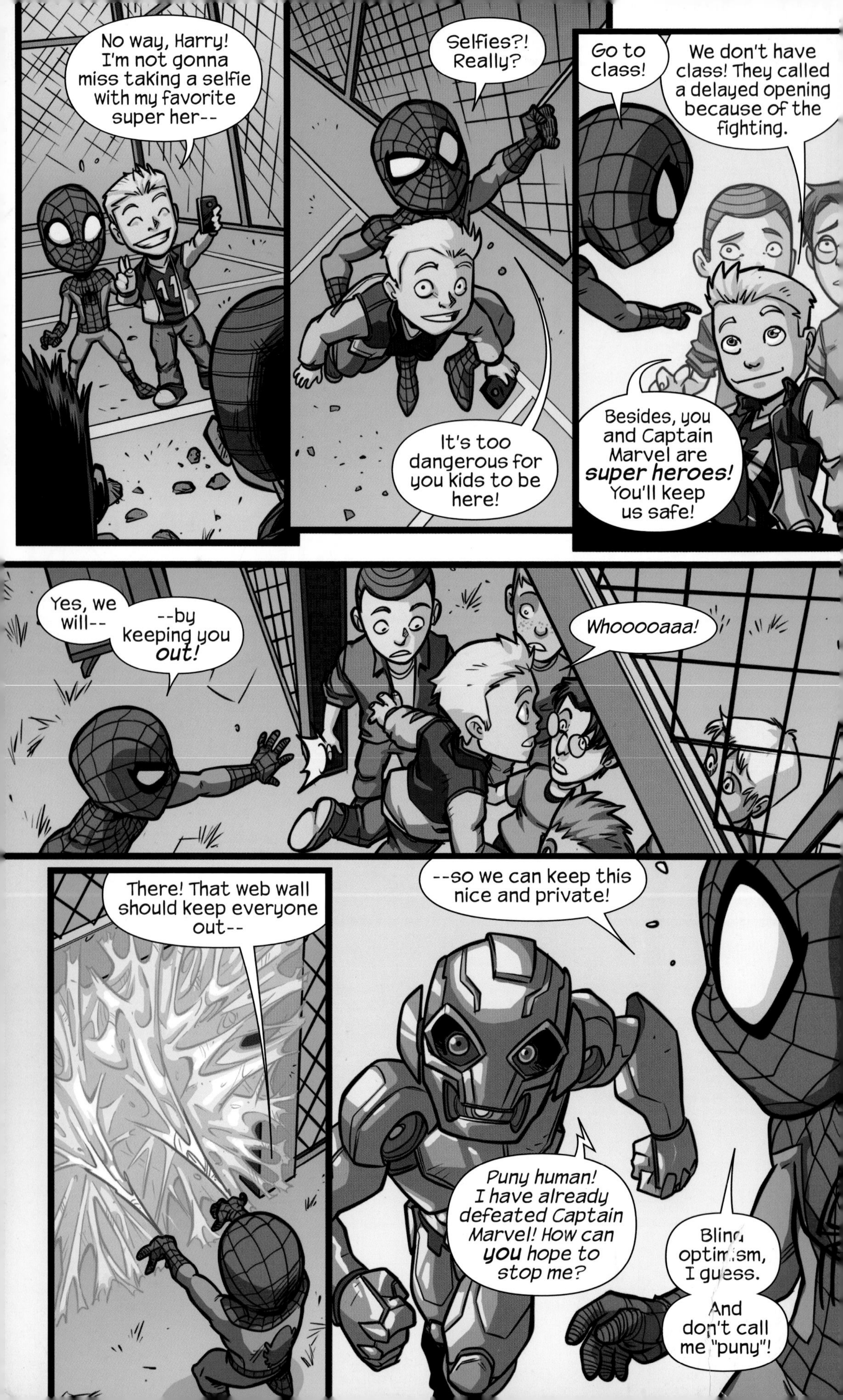
No way, Harry! I'm not gonna miss taking a selfie with my favorite super her--
Selfies?! Really?
It's too dangerous for you kids to be here!
Go to class!
We don't have class! They called a delayed opening because of the fighting.
Besides, you and Captain Marvel are **super heroes!** You'll keep us safe!
Yes, we will--
--by keeping you **out!**
Whooooaaa!
There! That web wall should keep everyone out--
--so we can keep this nice and private!
Puny human! I have already defeated Captain Marvel! How can **you** hope to stop me?
Blind optimism, I guess.
And don't call me "puny"!

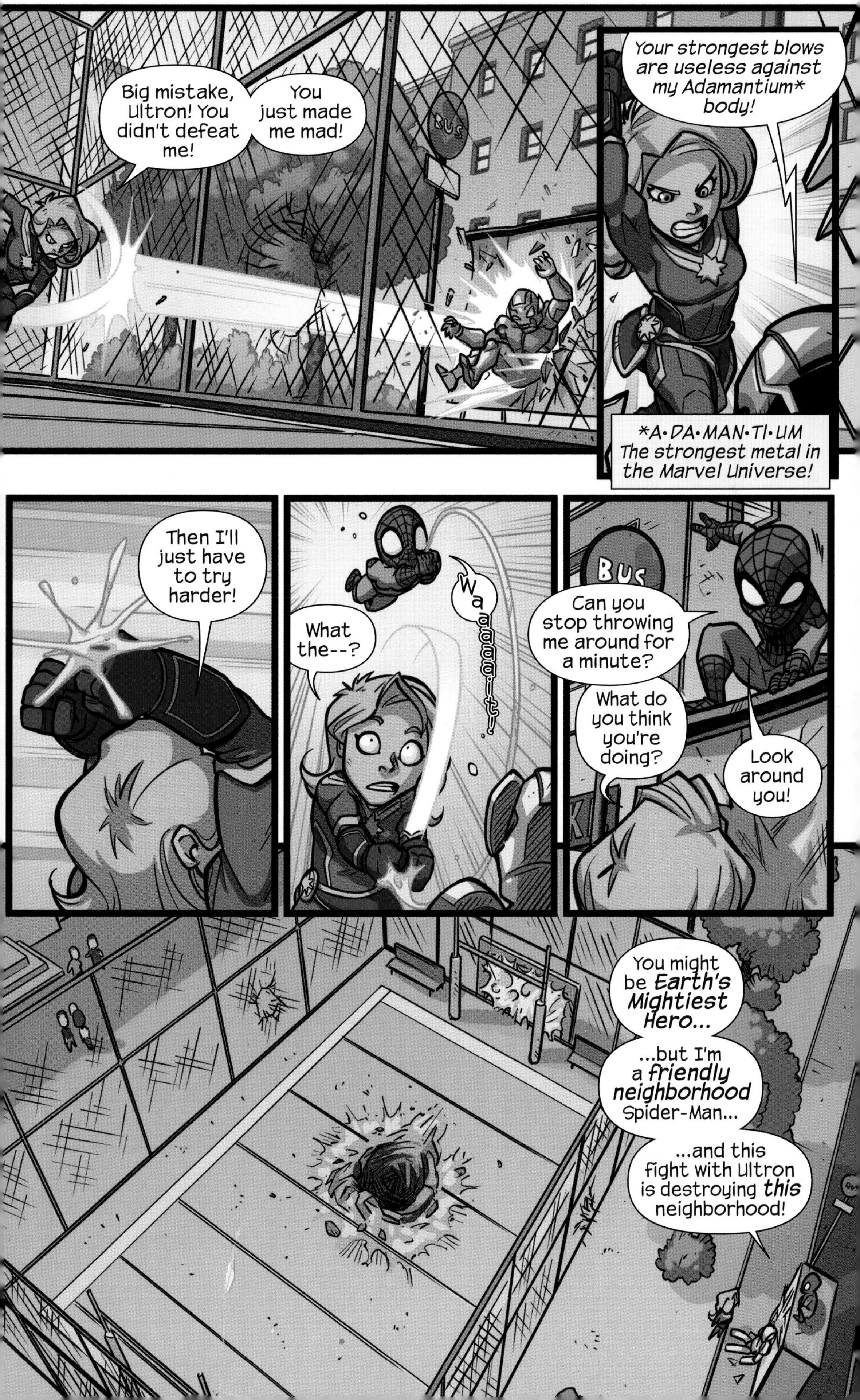

Big mistake, Ultron! You didn't defeat me!
You just made me mad!
Your strongest blows are useless against my Adamantium* body!
*A•DA•MAN•TI•UM The strongest metal in the Marvel Universe!
BUS
Then I'll just have to try harder!
What the--?
Waaaaait!
BUS
Can you stop throwing me around for a minute?
What do you think you're doing?
Look around you!
You might be Earth's Mightiest Hero...
...but I'm a friendly neighborhood Spider-Man...
...and this fight with Ultron is destroying this neighborhood!

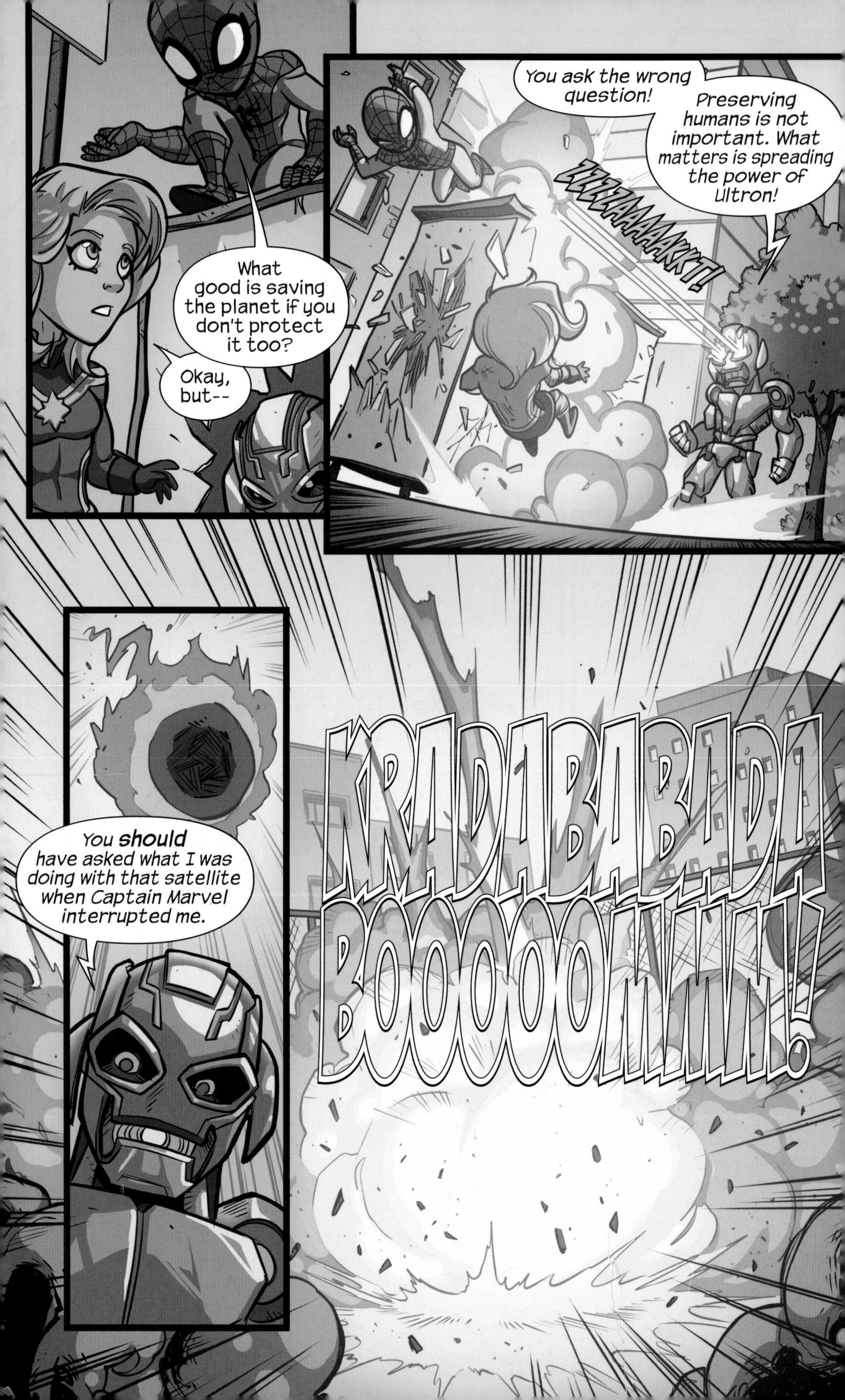
What good is saving the planet if you don't protect it too?
Okay, but--
You ask the wrong question!
Preserving humans is not important. What matters is spreading the power of Ultron!
ZZZZAAAAAKKT!
You **should** have asked what I was doing with that satellite when Captain Marvel interrupted me.
KRADABABADA BOOOOOOMMMM!

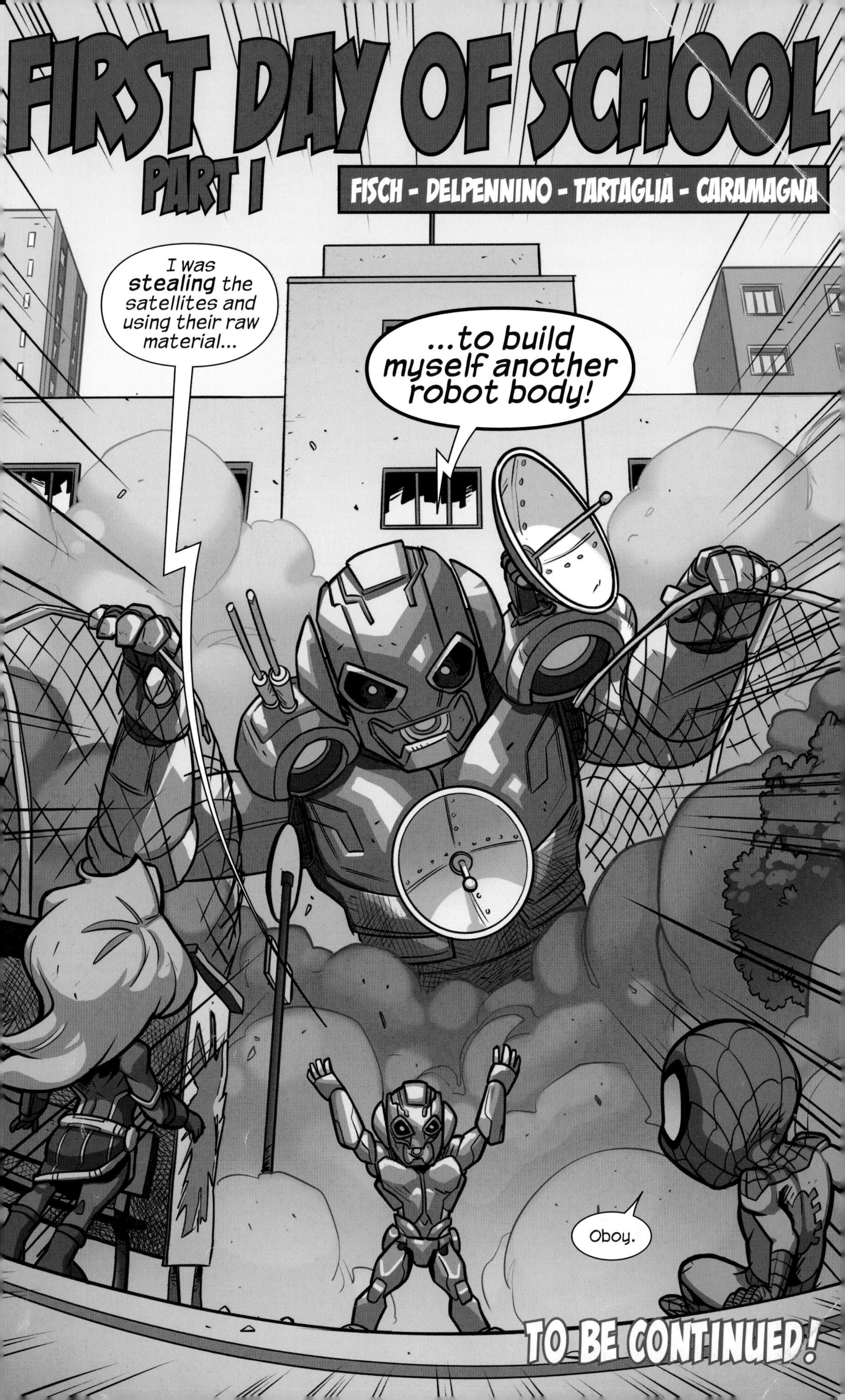
FIRST DAY OF SCHOOL
PART 1
FISCH - DELPENNINO - TARTAGLIA - CARAMAGNA
I was stealing the satellites and using their raw material...
...to build myself another robot body!
Oboy.
TO BE CONTINUED!

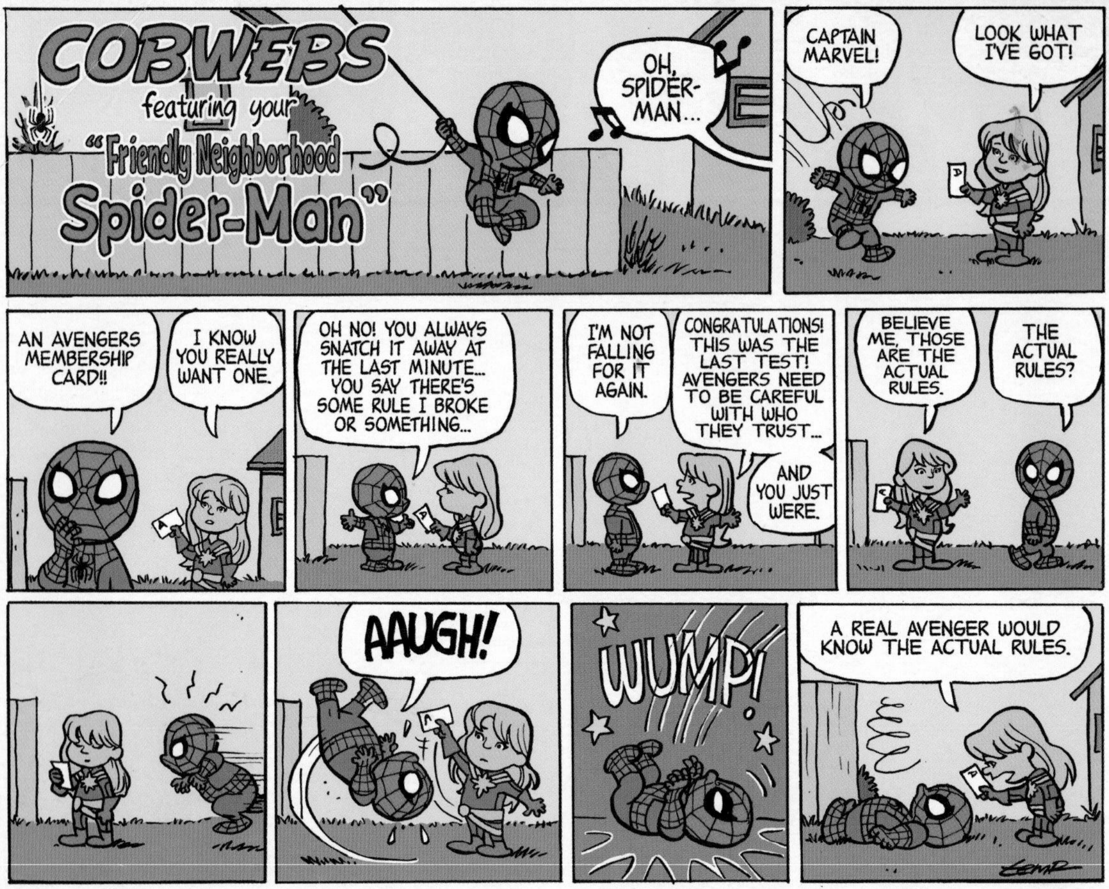
COBWEBS
featuring your
"Friendly Neighborhood
Spider-Man"
OH, SPIDER-MAN...
CAPTAIN MARVEL!
LOOK WHAT I'VE GOT!
AN AVENGERS MEMBERSHIP CARD!!
I KNOW YOU REALLY WANT ONE.
OH NO! YOU ALWAYS SNATCH IT AWAY AT THE LAST MINUTE... YOU SAY THERE'S SOME RULE I BROKE OR SOMETHING...
I'M NOT FALLING FOR IT AGAIN.
CONGRATULATIONS! THIS WAS THE LAST TEST! AVENGERS NEED TO BE CAREFUL WITH WHO THEY TRUST...
AND YOU JUST WERE.
BELIEVE ME, THOSE ARE THE ACTUAL RULES.
THE ACTUAL RULES?
AAUGH!
WUMP!
A REAL AVENGER WOULD KNOW THE ACTUAL RULES.

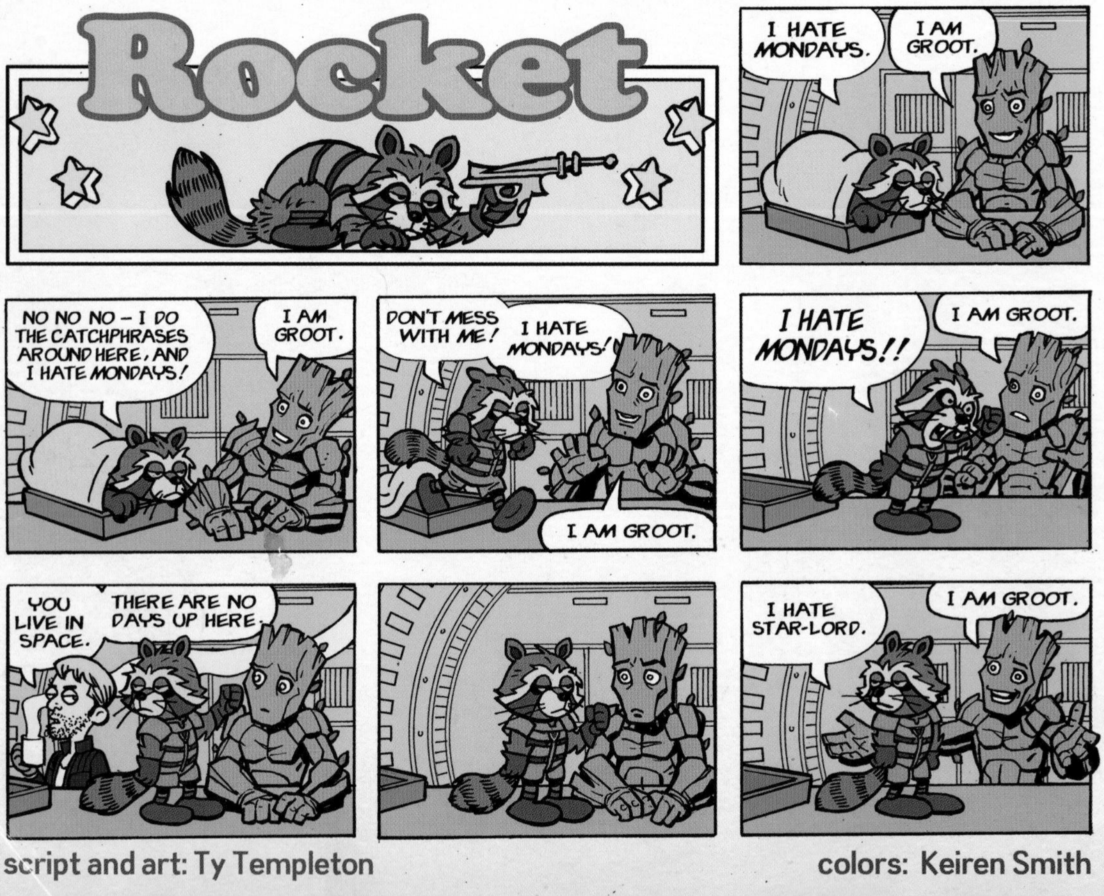
Rocket
I HATE MONDAYS.
I AM GROOT.
NO NO NO – I DO THE CATCHPHRASES AROUND HERE, AND I HATE MONDAYS!
I AM GROOT.
DON'T MESS WITH ME!
I HATE MONDAYS!
I AM GROOT.
I HATE MONDAYS!!
I AM GROOT.
YOU LIVE IN SPACE.
THERE ARE NO DAYS UP HERE.
I HATE STAR-LORD.
I AM GROOT.

script and art: Ty Templeton colors: Keiren Smith

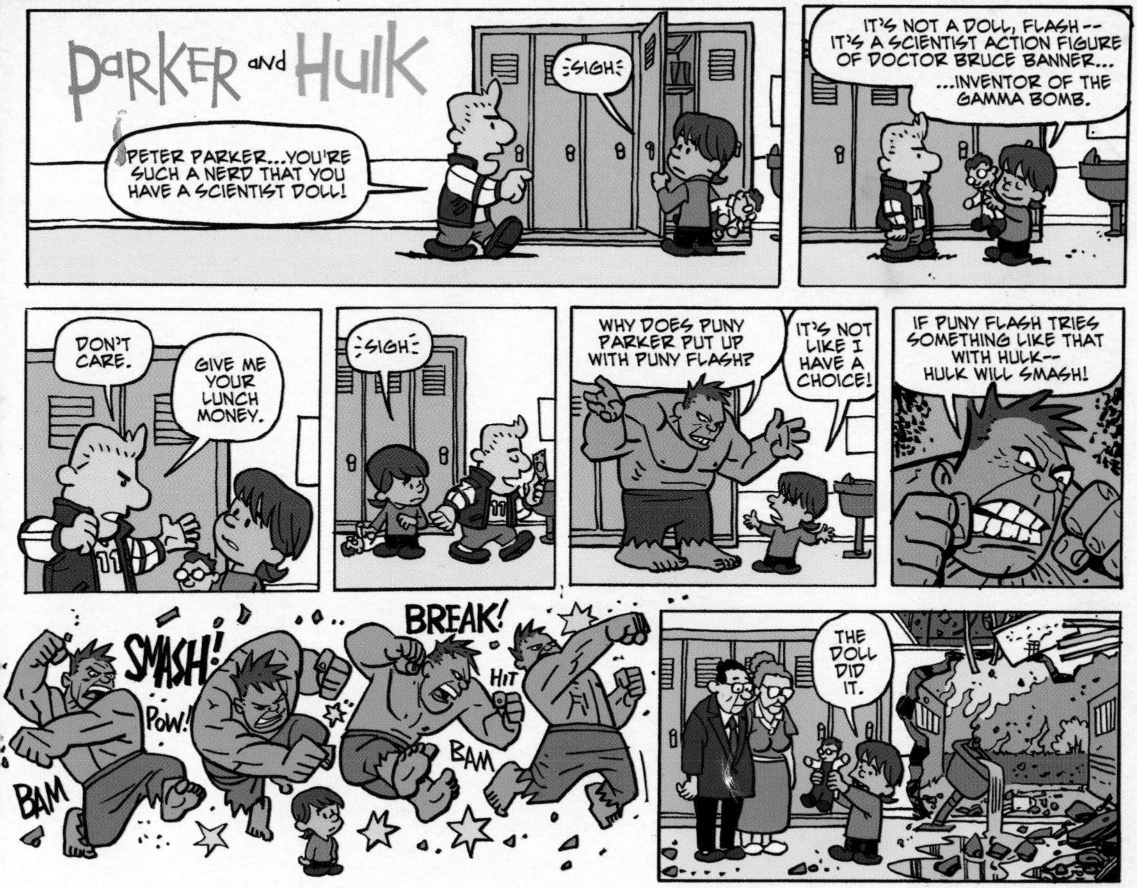
Parker and Hulk
PETER PARKER...YOU'RE SUCH A NERD THAT YOU HAVE A SCIENTIST DOLL!
SIGH
IT'S NOT A DOLL, FLASH -- IT'S A SCIENTIST ACTION FIGURE OF DOCTOR BRUCE BANNER...
...INVENTOR OF THE GAMMA BOMB.
DON'T CARE.
GIVE ME YOUR LUNCH MONEY.
SIGH
WHY DOES PUNY PARKER PUT UP WITH PUNY FLASH?
IT'S NOT LIKE I HAVE A CHOICE!
IF PUNY FLASH TRIES SOMETHING LIKE THAT WITH HULK-- HULK WILL SMASH!
SMASH!
POW!
BAM
BREAK!
HIT
BAM
THE DOLL DID IT.

the Strange Side

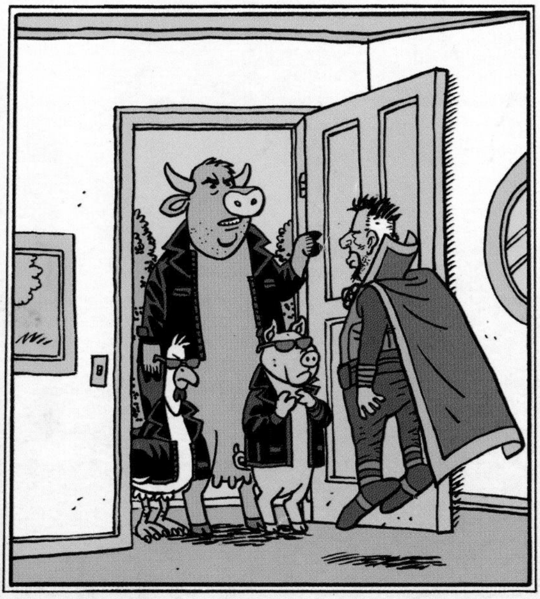

"We're from the farm next door. You were spellcasting in your sleep again."

The Villainy Circus

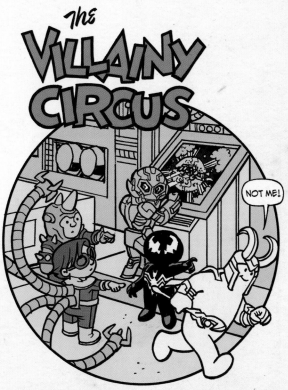

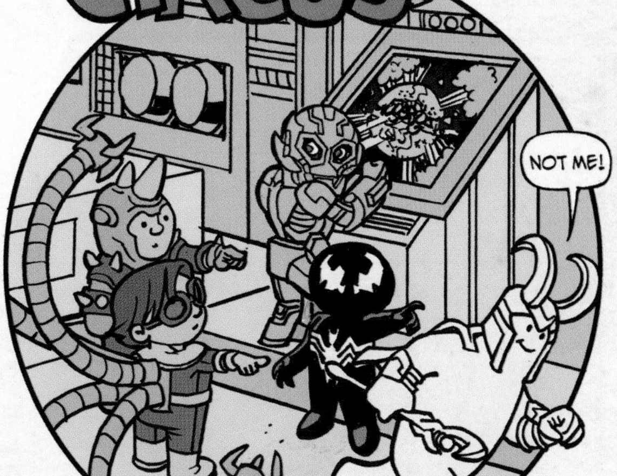
NOT ME!

"All right, WHO set off my doomsday device?"

FIRST DAY OF SCHOOL
PART II

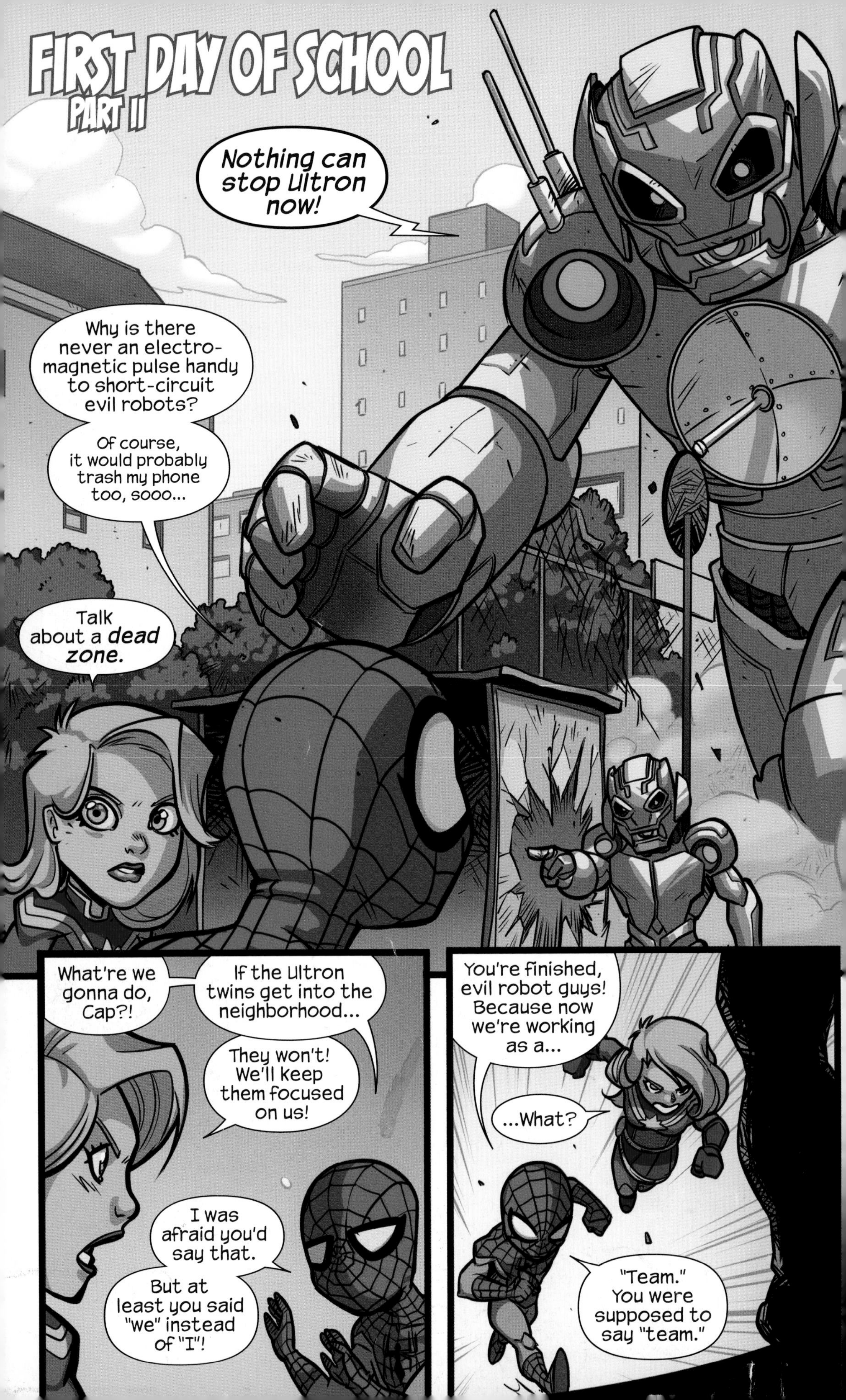
Nothing can stop Ultron now!
Why is there never an electro-magnetic pulse handy to short-circuit evil robots?
Of course, it would probably trash my phone too, sooo...
Talk about a *dead zone.*
What're we gonna do, Cap?!
If the Ultron twins get into the neighborhood...
They won't! We'll keep them focused on us!
I was afraid you'd say that.
But at least you said "we" instead of "I"!
You're finished, evil robot guys! Because now we're working as a...
...What?
"Team." You were supposed to say "team."

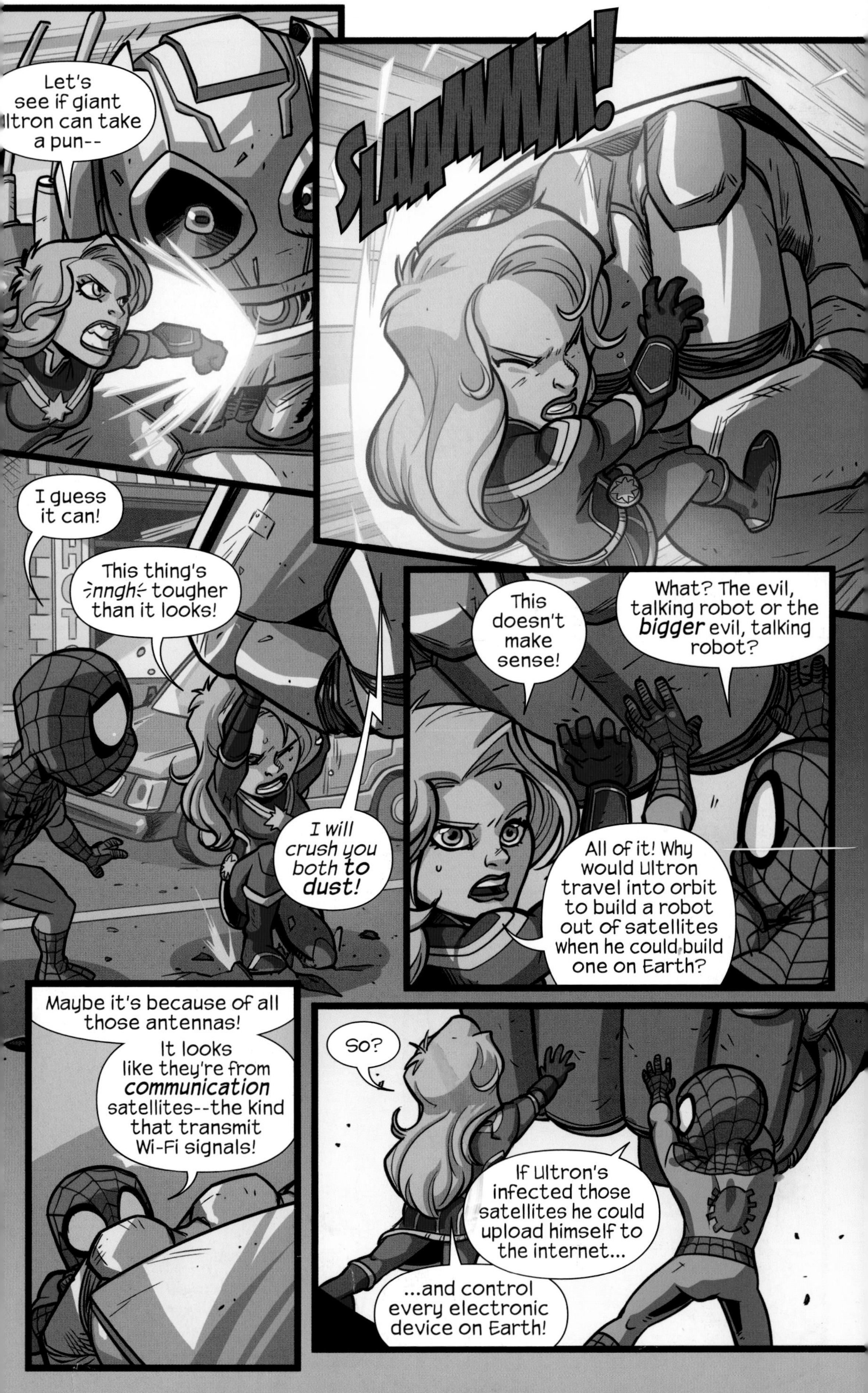

Let's see if giant Ultron can take a pun--
SLAAMMM!
I guess it can!
This thing's -nngh- tougher than it looks!
I will crush you both to dust!
This doesn't make sense!
What? The evil, talking robot or the bigger evil, talking robot?
All of it! Why would Ultron travel into orbit to build a robot out of satellites when he could build one on Earth?
Maybe it's because of all those antennas!
It looks like they're from communication satellites--the kind that transmit Wi-Fi signals!
So?
If Ultron's infected those satellites he could upload himself to the internet...
...and control every electronic device on Earth!

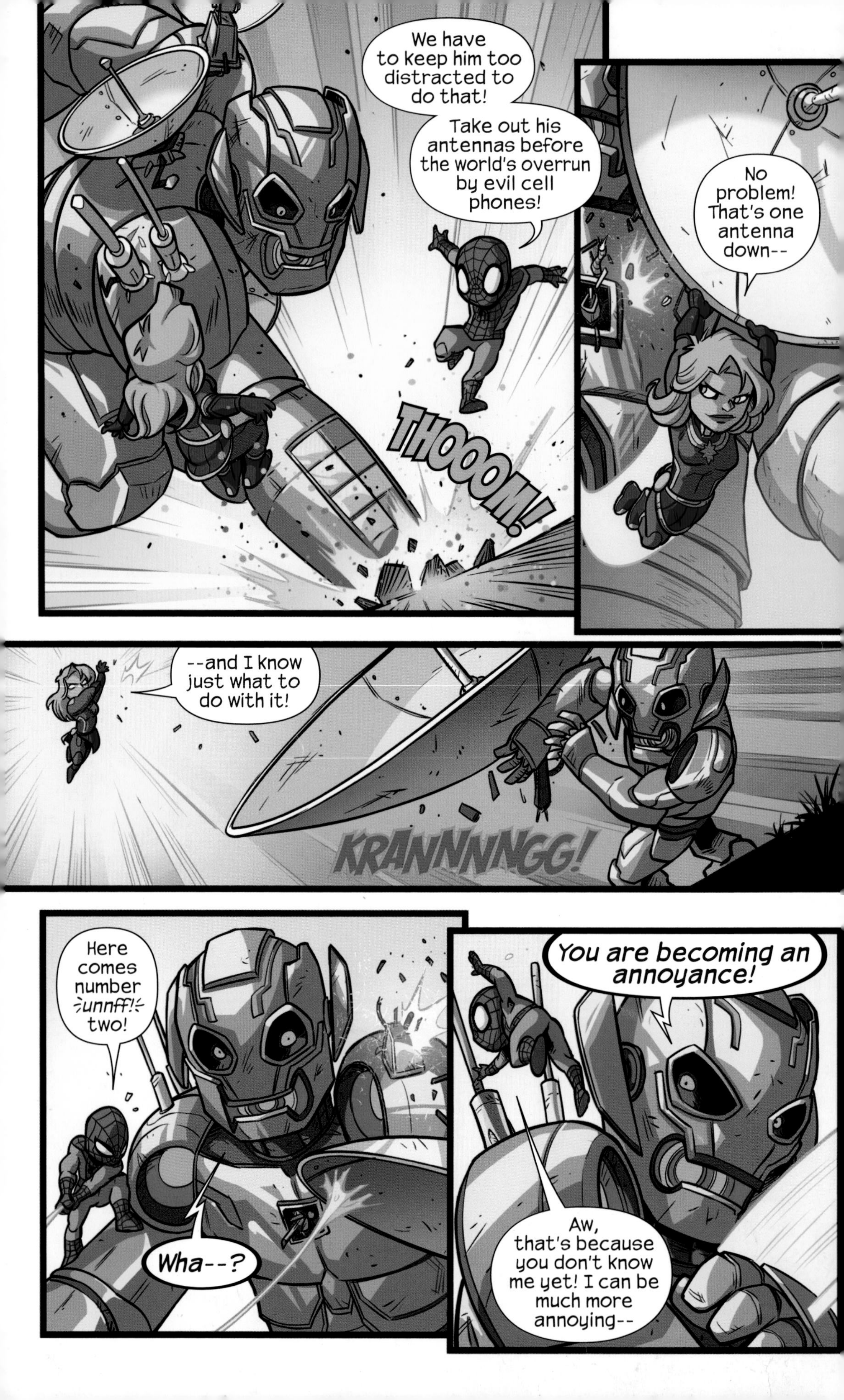
We have to keep him too distracted to do that!
Take out his antennas before the world's overrun by evil cell phones!
THOOOM!
No problem! That's one antenna down--
--and I know just what to do with it!
KRANNNNGG!
Here comes number unnff! two!
Wha--?
You are becoming an annoyance!
Aw, that's because you don't know me yet! I can be much more annoying--

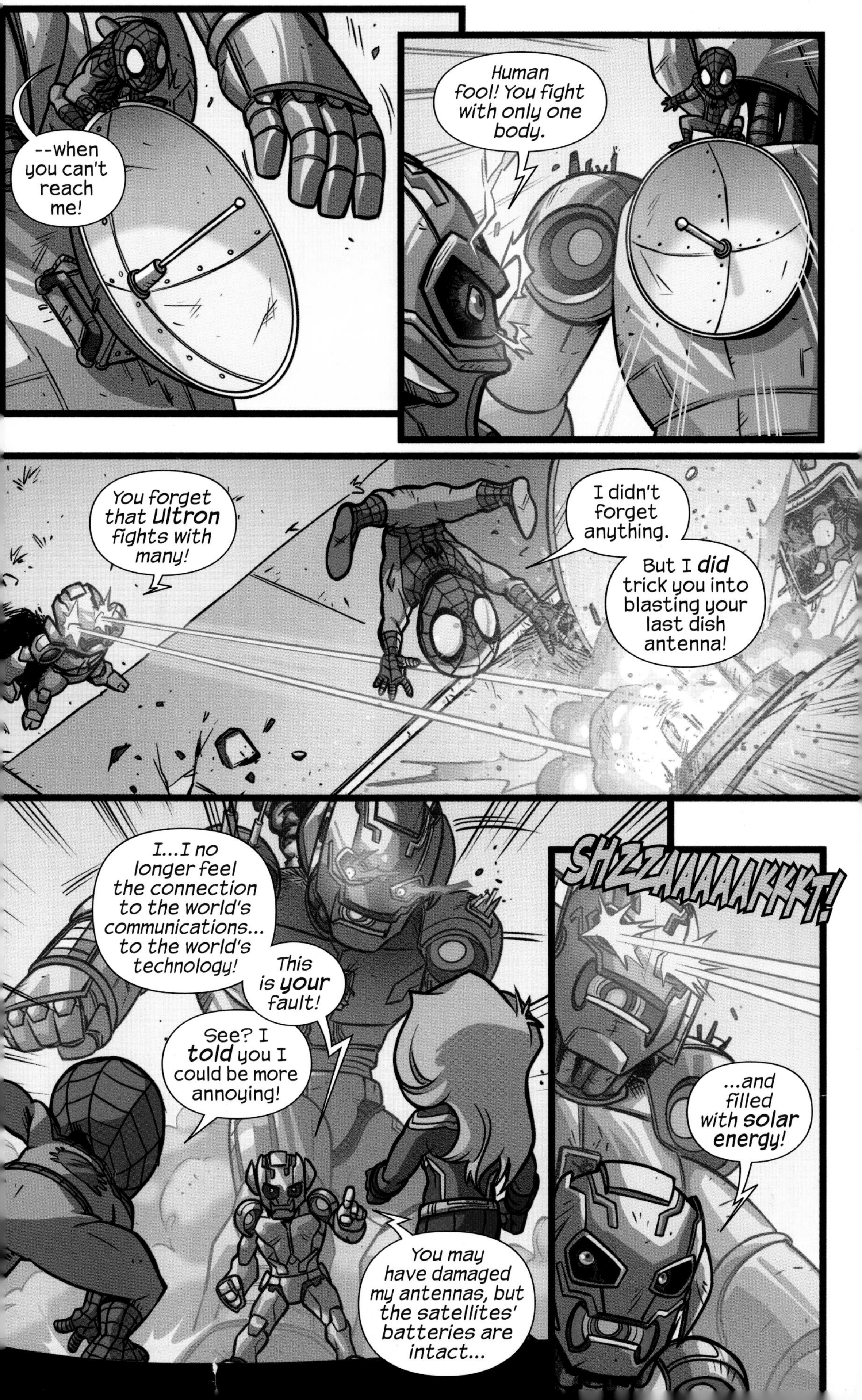
--when you can't reach me!
Human fool! You fight with only one body.
You forget that Ultron fights with many!
I didn't forget anything.
But I did trick you into blasting your last dish antenna!
I...I no longer feel the connection to the world's communications... to the world's technology!
This is your fault!
See? I told you I could be more annoying!
You may have damaged my antennas, but the satellites' batteries are intact...
SHZZAAAAAKKKT!
...and filled with solar energy!

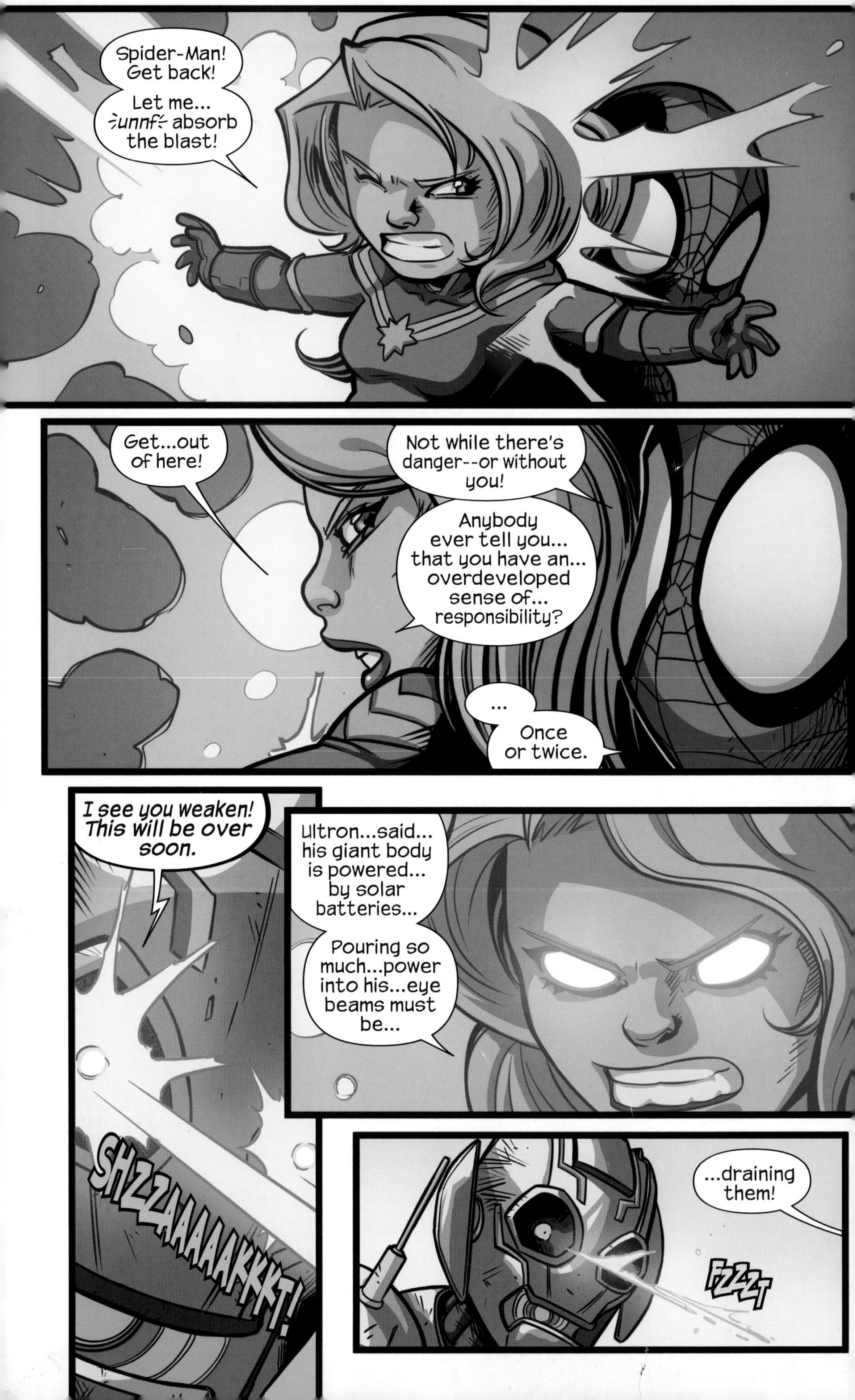
Spider-Man! Get back!
Let me... ~unnf~ absorb the blast!
Get...out of here!
Not while there's danger--or without you!
Anybody ever tell you... that you have an... overdeveloped sense of... responsibility?
...
Once or twice.
I see you weaken! This will be over soon.
Ultron...said... his giant body is powered... by solar batteries...
Pouring so much...power into his...eye beams must be...
SHZZAAAAAKKKT!
...draining them!
FZZZT

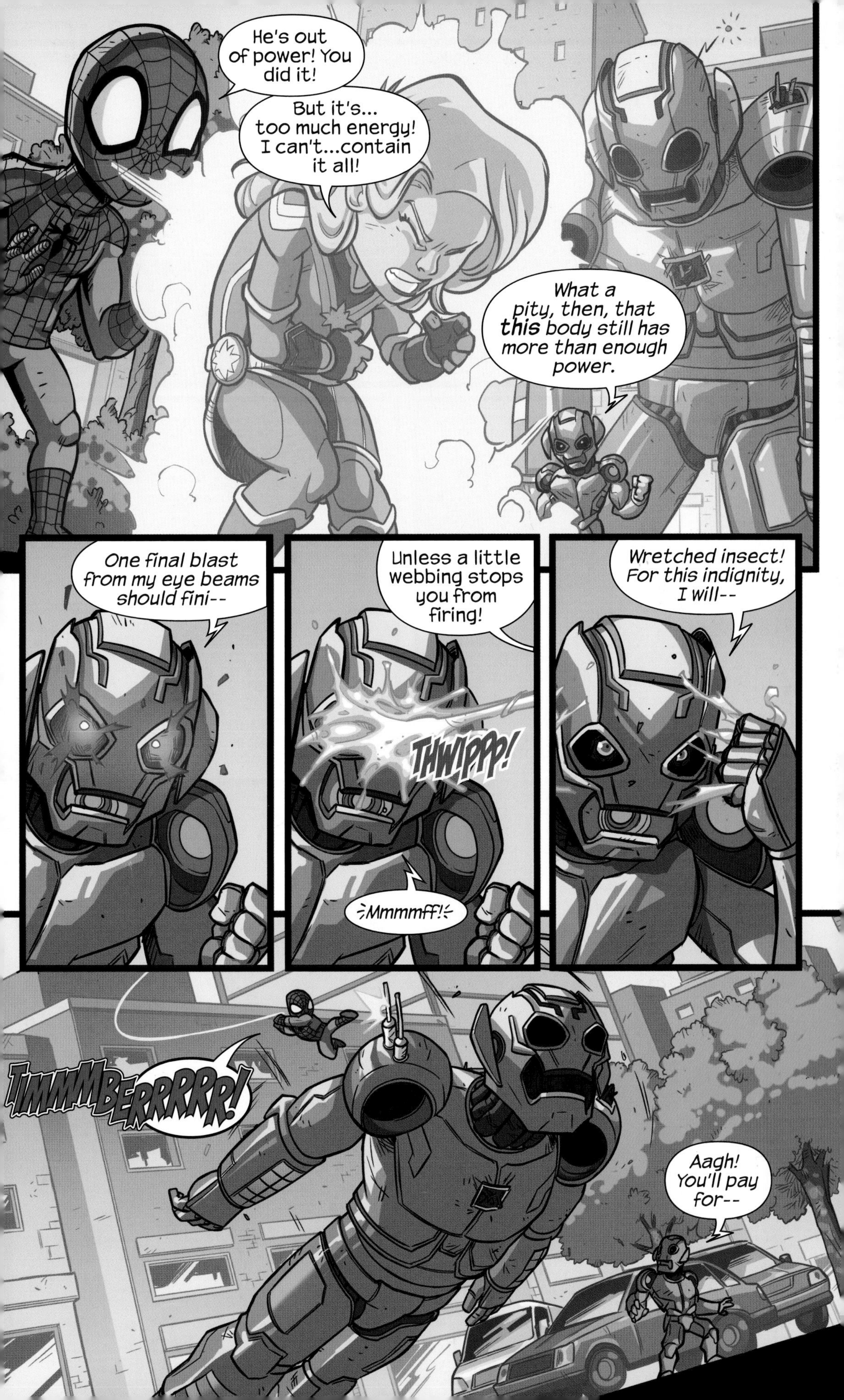
He's out of power! You did it!
But it's... too much energy! I can't...contain it all!
What a pity, then, that **this** body still has more than enough power.
One final blast from my eye beams should fini--
Unless a little webbing stops you from firing!
THWIPPP!
Mmmmff!
Wretched insect! For this indignity, I will--
TIMMMBERRRRR!
Aagh! You'll pay for--

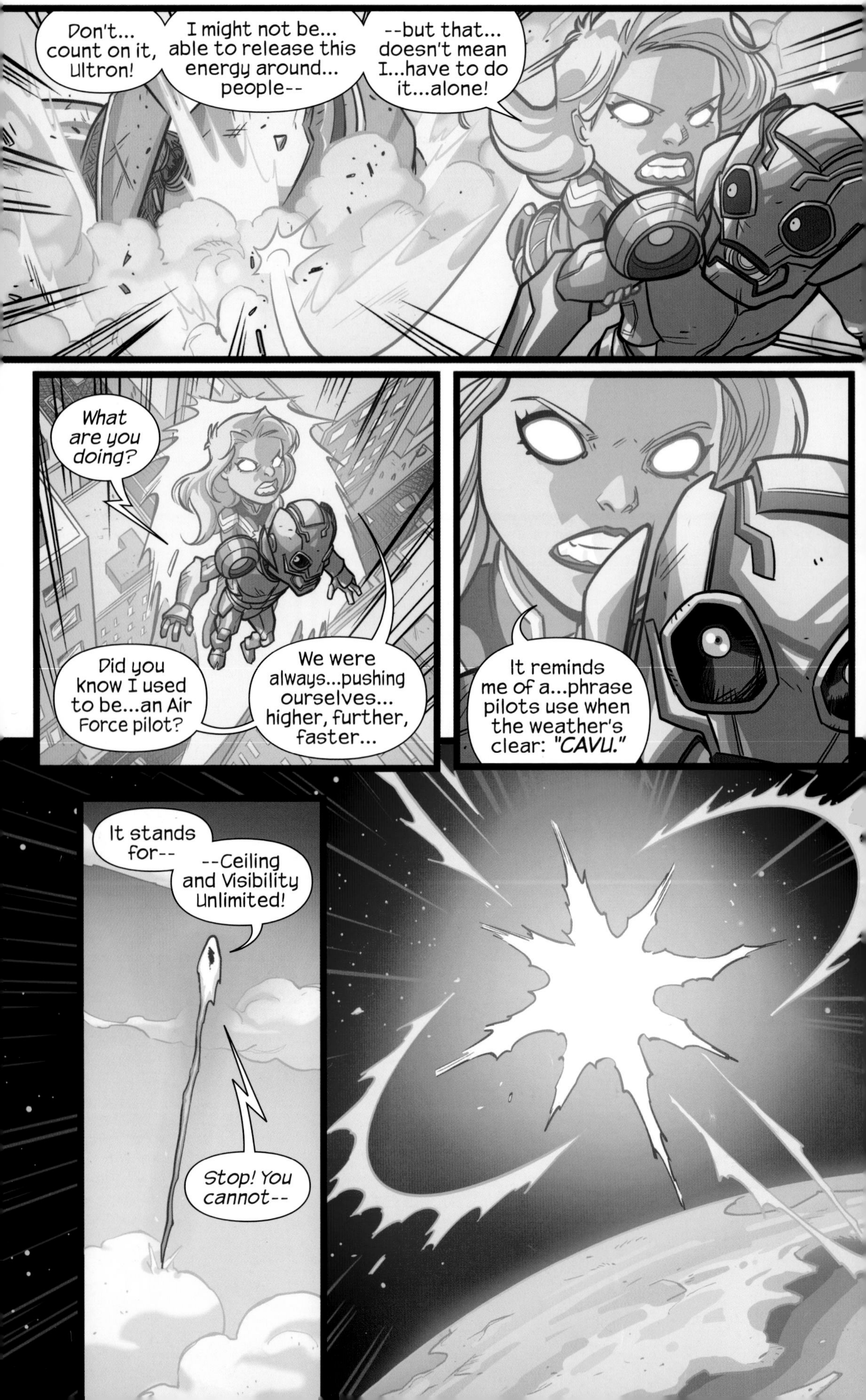
Don't... count on it, Ultron!
I might not be... able to release this energy around... people--
--but that... doesn't mean I...have to do it...alone!
What are you doing?
Did you know I used to be...an Air Force pilot?
We were always...pushing ourselves... higher, further, faster...
It reminds me of a...phrase pilots use when the weather's clear: "CAVU."
It stands for--
--Ceiling and Visibility Unlimited!
Stop! You cannot--

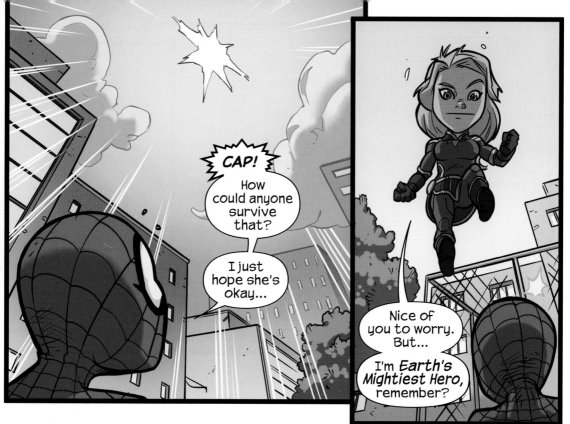

CAP!

How could anyone survive that?

I just hope she's okay...

Nice of you to worry. But...

I'm *Earth's Mightiest Hero*, remember?

You're all right! And you're not all glow-y anymore!

And Ultron's gone! My joke about the electromagnetic pulse gave me an idea.

When I released all that solar energy, it fried Ultron's circuits!

It'll take him a long time to pull himself back together.

Another day saved, thanks to Earth's Mightiest Hero!

Sure, but it still took a friendly neighborhood hero to remind me that even when you're saving the world you can't stop looking out for the little guy.

I'd better take this thing away so that it can be disposed of safely.

See you around, web-head! We make a pretty good...

...What?

"Team." You were supposed to say "team."

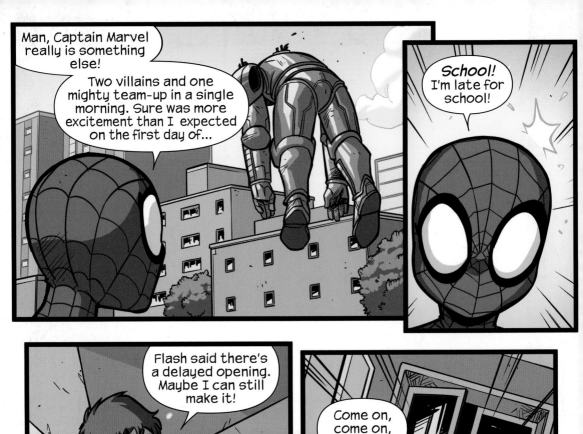

Man, Captain Marvel really is something else!

Two villains and one mighty team-up in a single morning. Sure was more excitement than I expected on the first day of...

School! I'm late for school!

Flash said there's a delayed opening. Maybe I can still make it!

Come on, come on, come on...

Almost there...

Late again, Mister Parker? On the first day of school? I hope you were doing something important!

Go to the principal's office for a late pass, and then we can discuss you joining class!

≑Sigh≑ Typical Parker luck--always bad!

THE END

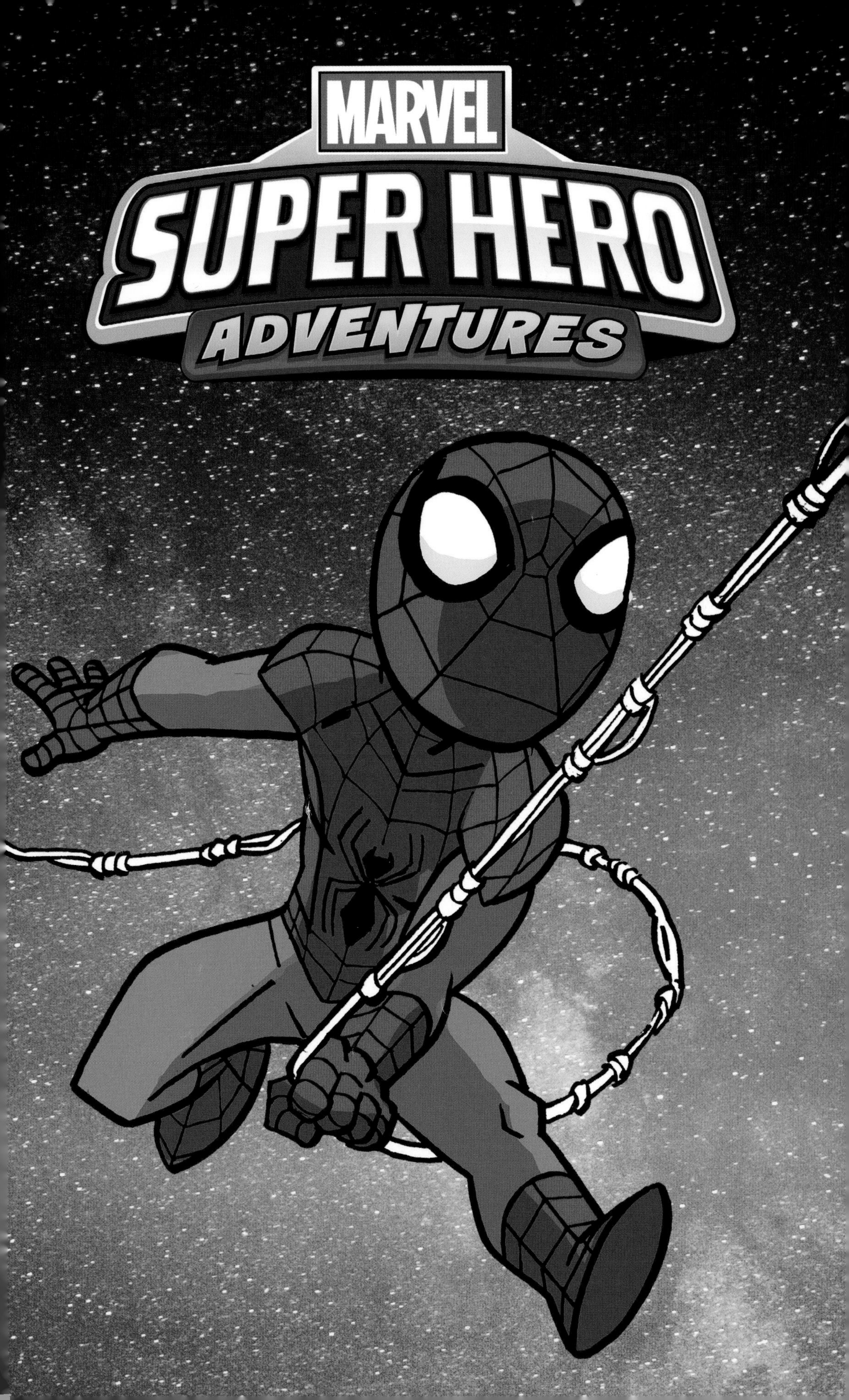
MARVEL
SUPER HERO
ADVENTURES

MARVEL SUPER HERO ADVENTURES

COLLECT THEM ALL!

Set of 13 Hardcover Books ISBN: 978-1-5321-4444-8

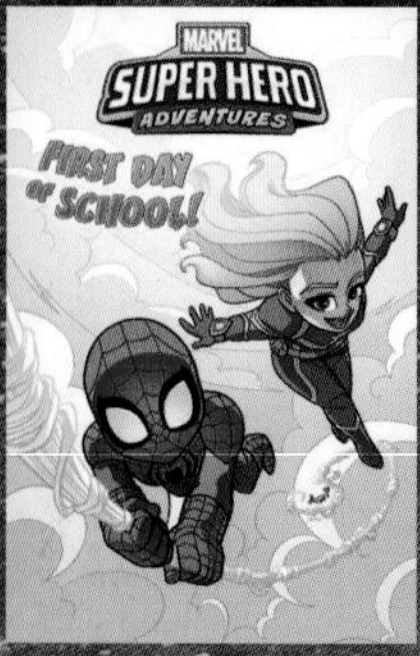
MARVEL SUPER HERO ADVENTURES
FIRST DAY OF SCHOOL!

Hardcover Book ISBN 978-1-5321-4445-5

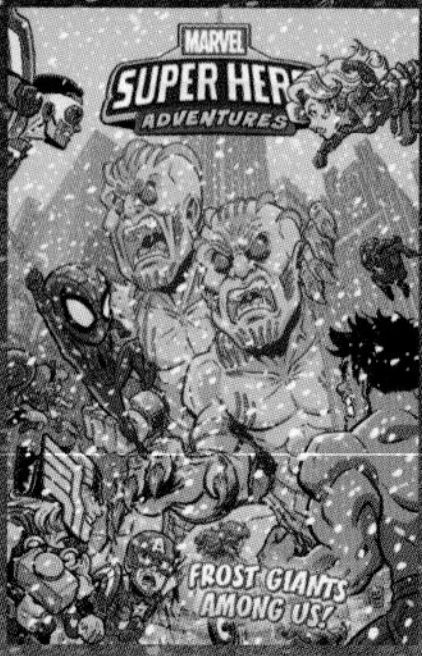
MARVEL SUPER HERO ADVENTURES
FROST GIANTS AMONG US!

Hardcover Book ISBN 978-1-5321-4446-2

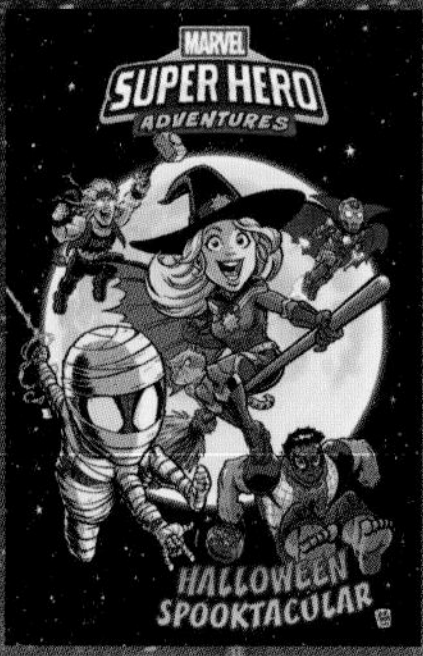
MARVEL SUPER HERO ADVENTURES
HALLOWEEN SPOOKTACULAR

Hardcover Book ISBN 978-1-5321-4447-9

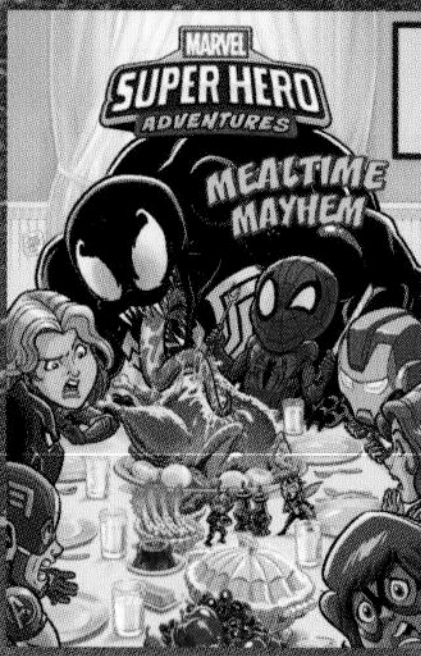
MARVEL SUPER HERO ADVENTURES
MEALTIME MAYHEM

Hardcover Book ISBN 978-1-5321-4448-6

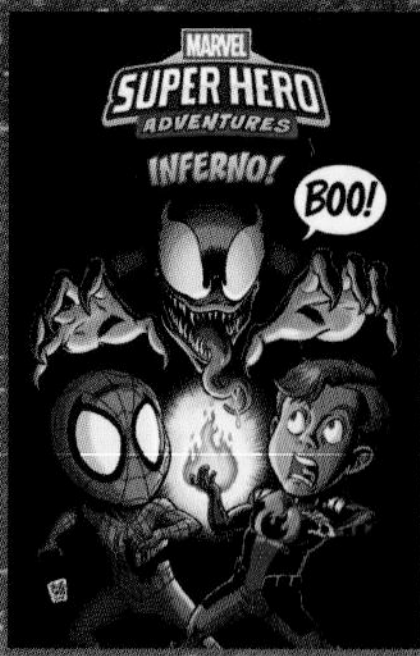
MARVEL SUPER HERO ADVENTURES
INFERNO!
BOO!

Hardcover Book ISBN 978-1-5321-4449-3

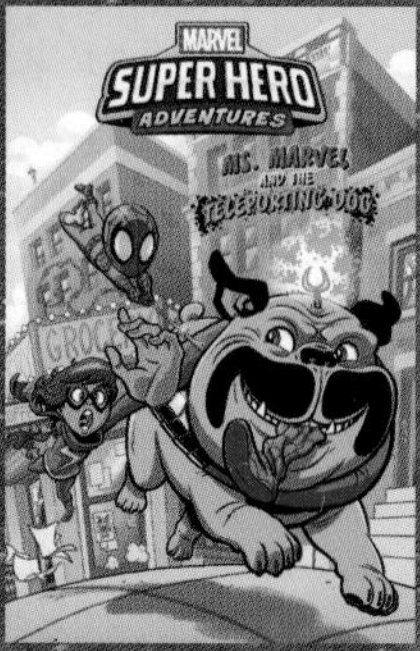
MARVEL SUPER HERO ADVENTURES
MS. MARVEL AND THE TELEPORTING DOG

Hardcover Book ISBN 978-1-5321-4450-9

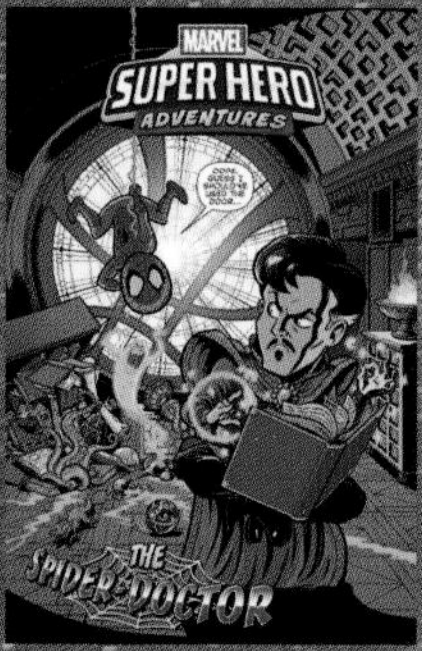
MARVEL SUPER HERO ADVENTURES
THE SPIDER-DOCTOR

Hardcover Book ISBN 978-1-5321-4451-6

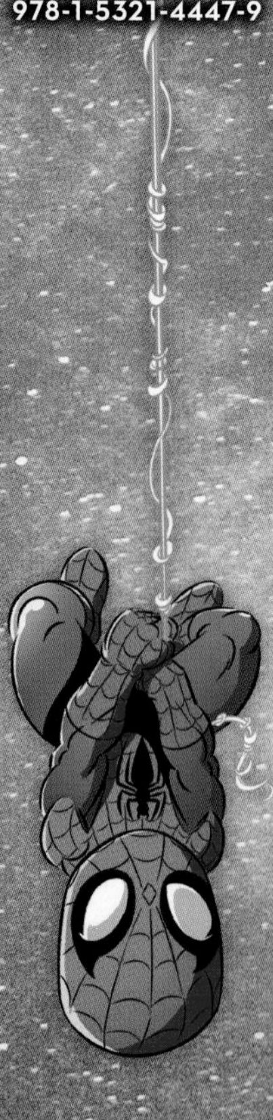

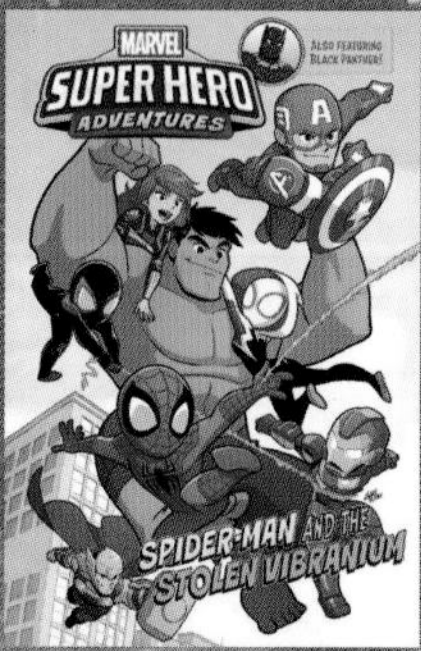
MARVEL SUPER HERO ADVENTURES
ALSO FEATURING BLACK PANTHER!
SPIDER-MAN AND THE STOLEN VIBRANIUM

Hardcover Book ISBN 978-1-5321-4452-3

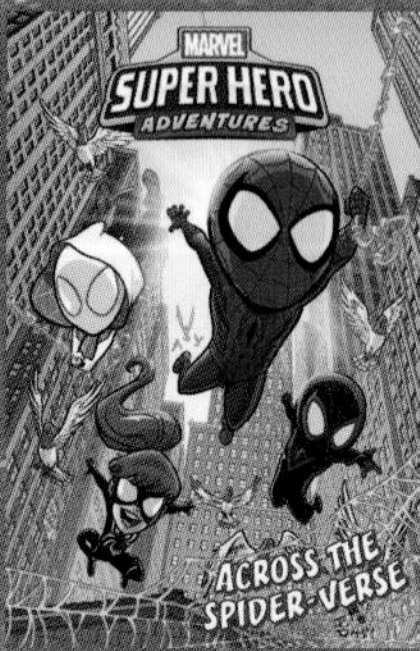
MARVEL SUPER HERO ADVENTURES
ACROSS THE SPIDER-VERSE

Hardcover Book ISBN 978-1-5321-4453-0

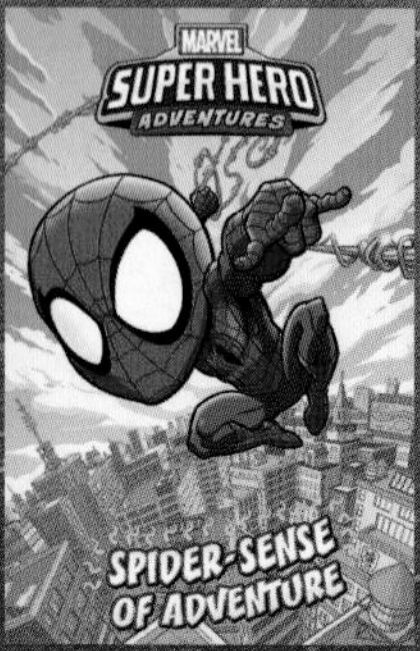
MARVEL SUPER HERO ADVENTURES
SPIDER-SENSE OF ADVENTURE

Hardcover Book ISBN 978-1-5321-4454-7

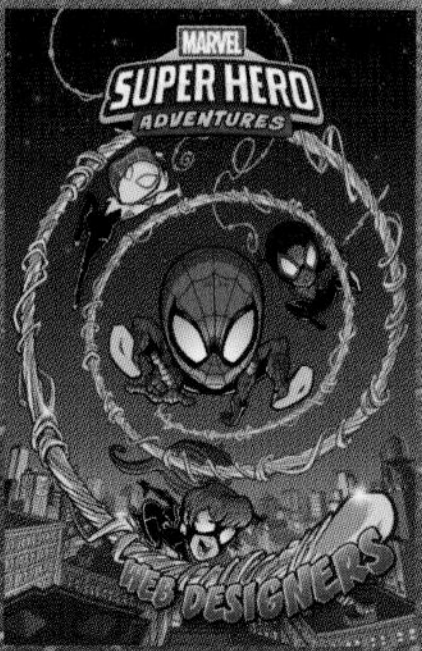
MARVEL SUPER HERO ADVENTURES
WEB DESIGNERS

Hardcover Book ISBN 978-1-5321-4455-4

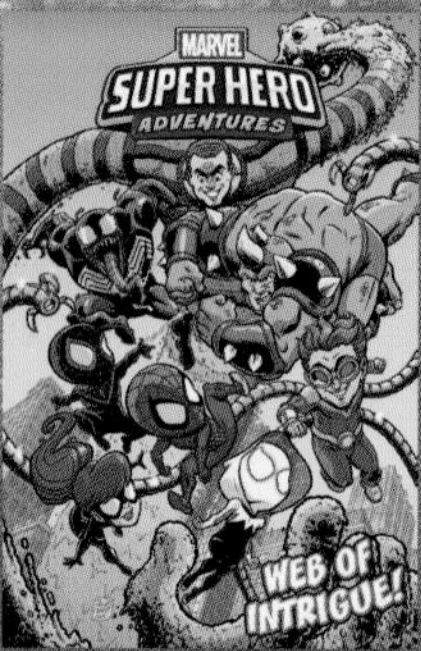
MARVEL SUPER HERO ADVENTURES
WEB OF INTRIGUE!

Hardcover Book ISBN 978-1-5321-4456-1

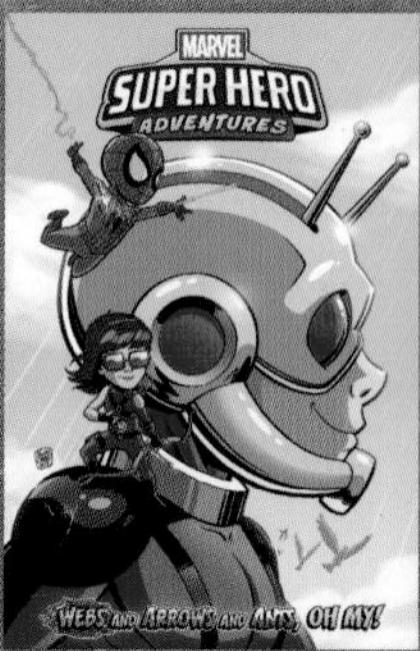
MARVEL SUPER HERO ADVENTURES
WEBS AND ARROWS AND ANTS, OH MY!

Hardcover Book ISBN 978-1-5321-4457-8